2

Catania Celine

Love Grammiè +

Grampiè

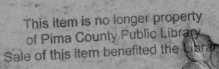

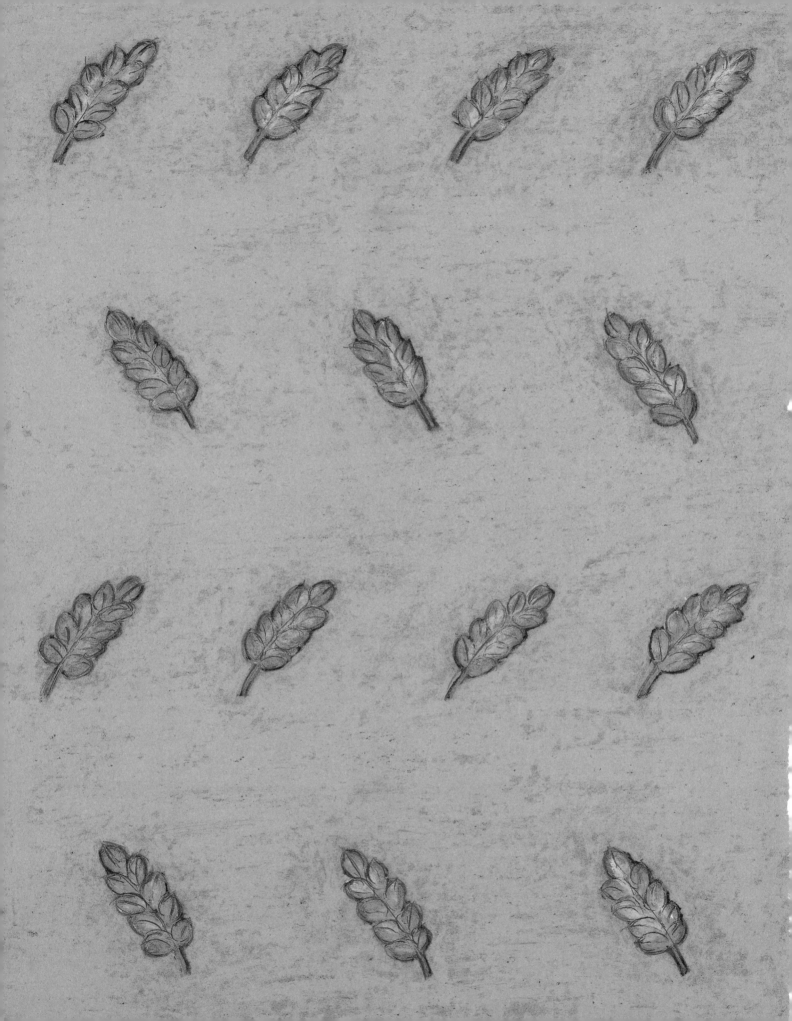

THE LITTLE RED HEN
and
THE EAR OF WHEAT

For my mother — M. F.
For Chris, Céline, Fiona and Dominique — E. B.

Barefoot Beginners
an imprint of
Barefoot Books, Inc.
41 Schermerhorn Street, Suite 145
Brooklyn, New York
11201-4845

This book is printed on 100% acid-free paper
Illustrations were prepared in watercolor pastel,
worked dry on 300gsm black card

Graphic design by Jennie Hoare, Bradford on Avon
Typeset in Futura Heavy 24pt
Color separation by Unifoto, Cape Town
Printed and bound in Singapore by Tien Wah Press (Pte) Ltd

ISBN 1 902283 47 3

1 3 5 7 9 8 6 4 2

THE LITTLE RED HEN
and
THE EAR OF WHEAT

written by MARY FINCH • illustrated by ELISABETH BELL

BAREFOOT BOOKS

Once upon a time
there lived a rooster
and a mouse and a
little red hen in a
small brown house
with a red roof.

One day the little red hen
found a grain of wheat
lying on the ground.
"Look what I've found,"
she said to the rooster
and the mouse.

"I shall plant it in the soil.
Who will help me?"
"Not I," said the rooster.
"Not I," said the mouse.
"Then I'll do it myself,"
said the little red hen.

She scratched at the soil
and planted the grain.
"Who will help me water it?"
"Not I," said the rooster.
"Not I," said the mouse.
"Then I'll do it myself,"
said the little red hen.

She watered the soil and waited
for the wheat to grow. The sun shone,
and the wheat grew tall and straight.

When the ear of wheat
was golden, she said:
"Who will help me harvest it?"
"Not I," said the rooster.
"Not I," said the mouse.
"Then I'll do it myself,"
said the little red hen.

She picked the ear of wheat
and put it in a basket.
"Who will help me take it to
the mill to be ground into flour?"

"Not I," said the rooster.
"Not I," said the mouse.
"Then I'll do it myself,"
said the little red hen.

The miller ground the ear of wheat into fine white flour. "Who will help me make this flour into dough?"

"Not I," said the rooster.
"Not I," said the mouse.
"Then I'll do it myself,"
said the little red hen.

She mixed the flour into warm, yeasty dough. "Who will help me knead this dough into bread?"

"Not I," said the rooster.
"Not I," said the mouse.
"Then I'll do it myself,"
said the little red hen.

She made the dough
into a round, shiny loaf.
"Who will help me put
this loaf into the oven?"

"Not I," said the rooster.
"Not I," said the mouse.
"Then I'll do it myself,"
said the little red hen.

She put the loaf into
the oven to bake.
When it was ready,
she took out the
brown, crusty loaf.

"Who will help me eat
this warm fresh bread?"
"I will," said the rooster.
"I will," said the mouse.

"No, you won't,"
said the little red hen.
"I shall eat it myself,"
said the little red hen.
And she did.

"Oh," said the rooster.
"Oh," said the mouse.
"You didn't help me,"
said the little red hen.
"So I ate it myself,"
said the little red hen.

But the next time the little red hen found a grain of wheat lying on the ground,

the rooster scratched
at the soil and
planted the grain,

the mouse
watered
the soil,

and together the rooster
and the mouse and
the little red hen
watched the wheat
grow tall and straight.

Together they took the wheat to the mill to be ground, and together they made the flour into dough.

And when the dough was cooked, the rooster and the mouse and the little red hen sat down together and ate the nice, warm bread — and it was delicious!

HOW TO BAKE A WHOLEWHEAT LOAF

It is easy to bake your own bread. Homemade bread smells wonderful and tastes delicious. To make a wholewheat loaf like the little red hen's, you will need:

Ingredients

4 cups wholewheat flour
2 level teaspoonfuls salt
2 level teaspoonfuls sugar
1 tablespoon lard
1 tablespoon dried yeast
1 1/2 cups tepid water

Equipment

a sieve
a large mixing bowl
a small mixing bowl
a saucepan or kettle
a pint measuring jug
a wooden spoon

a teaspoon
a tablespoon
a kitchen towel
a metal baking sheet
a small, sharp knife

Method

1. Before you start, have all your ingredients and equipment ready. Bread rises best in a warm, draft-free room, so make sure that the mixing bowls are warm and that you have warm hands.

2. Sift the flour, salt and sugar through the sieve into the large mixing bowl.

3. Rub in the lard with your fingertips.

4. Put the yeast into the small mixing bowl. Heat the water in a saucepan or kettle until it is tepid; it must not be too hot. Pour about two tablespoons of water onto the yeast, then blend the yeast and water together with a teaspoon. Leave the mixture for five minutes. After this time it should start to bubble; this shows that the yeast is alive. Now stir in the rest of the water.

5. Make a well in the middle of the flour and stir in the water and yeast mixture with a wooden spoon. Then use your hands to work the mixture into a soft dough that leaves the sides of the bowl clean. If your hands get very sticky dip them in some more flour.

6. Turn the dough onto a floured surface and knead it for about ten minutes until it is smooth and elastic.

7. Shape the dough into a round loaf and place it on a lightly greased metal baking sheet. Use the knife to cut a slit or a cross on the top of the loaf.

8. Cover the loaf with a kitchen towel and leave it in a warm place, free from draft, for about 40 minutes until it has doubled in size. While you are waiting for it to rise, preheat the oven to 450° F. The oven will get very hot so make sure that you have a grown-up with you before you open it. To test that the loaf is ready to bake, press it lightly with a floured finger. If it springs back into shape, it is ready. Brush the top of the loaf lightly with a little milk or water.

9. Bake the loaf for about 30-40 minutes until it is well risen and a rich brown. To check if it is cooked, tap the bottom of it with your knuckles (be careful — it will be hot). It should sound hollow if it is ready. Remove the loaf from the baking sheet and leave to cool on a wire rack.

BAREFOOT BOOKS publishes high-quality picture books for children of all ages and specializes in the work of artists and writers from many cultures. If you have enjoyed this book and would like to receive a copy of our current catalog, please contact our New York office —
tel: 718 260 8946   fax: 1 888 346 9138 (toll free)
e-mail: ussales@barefoot-books.com
website: www.barefoot-books.com

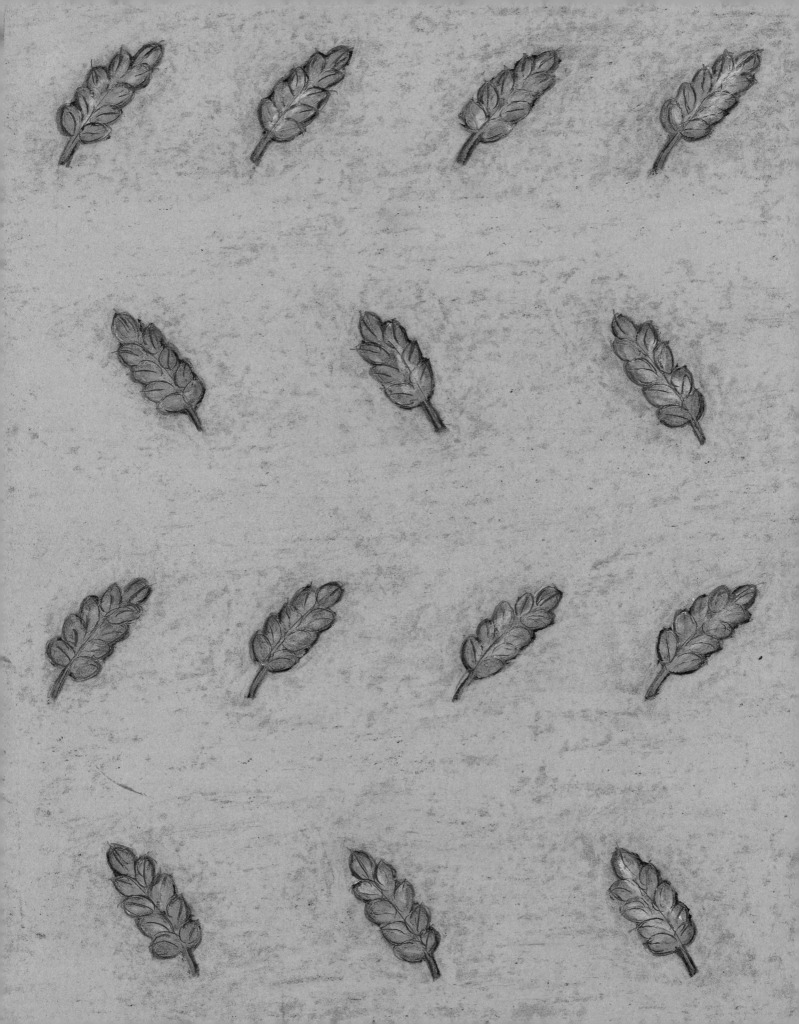